Louis A. Roberts

High Art: Pictures from the Poets, and Other Notions

Anatiposi

Louis A. Roberts

High Art: Pictures from the Poets, and Other Notions

Reprint of the original, first published in 1872.

1st Edition 2023 | ISBN: 978-3-38212-768-8

Anatiposi Verlag is an imprint of Outlook Verlagsgesellschaft mbH.

Verlag (Publisher): Outlook Verlag GmbH, Zeilweg 44, 60439 Frankfurt, Deutschland
Vertretungsberechtigt (Authorized to represent): E. Roepke, Zeilweg 44, 60439 Frankfurt, Deutschland
Druck (Print): Books on Demand GmbH, In de Tarpen 42, 22848 Norderstedt, Deutschland

HIGH ART:

ICTURES FROM The Poets,

AND OTHER NOTIONS.

BY

LOUIS A. ROBERTS.

" *The Poet's eye, in a fine frenzy rolling,*
Doth glance from heaven to earth, from earth to heaven,
And as imagination bodies forth
The forms of things unknown, the poet's pen
Turns them to shape, and gives to airy nothing
A local habitation and a name."

———— •━• ————

SPRINGFIELD, MASS.
D. E. FISK & COMPANY.

JAS. B. RODGERS CO.,
BOOK AND JOB PRINTERS,
PHILADELPHIA.

THE PUBLISHER'S NOTE.

HIGH ART.

7

TOO THIN.

"*Ladies and Gentlemen:—I regret to announce that, owing to a sudden and severe attack of illness, the gentleman who was advertised to take the part of Hamlet this evening, will be unable to appear before you. With the omission of this* **unimportant** *character, however, the play will begin as usual—with all our splendid scenic effects, including a real ghost. Hoping, ladies and gentlemen, that this little circumstance will in nowise detract from your pleasure in the evening's entertainment, the performance will now commence.*"

8

When Freedom from her mountain height
   Unfurled her standard to the air,
She tore the azure robe of night,
   And set the stars of glory there.

JOSEPH RODMAN DRAKE.

There studious let me sit,
And hold high converse with the mighty
dead.

ThOMSON.

Gay birds in cages pining,
　　Are not the birds for me;
The plumes so brightly shining,
　　I care not now to see;
But I've a bird—

THOMAS HAYNES BAYLY—
"THE ROSE THAT ALL ARE PRAISING."

The most unkindest cut of all!

SHAKSPEARE.

Over the river they beckon to me,
 Loved ones who've crossed to the
  further side;
The gleam of their snowy robes I see,
 But their voices are lost in the rushing
  tide.

NANCY A. W. PRIEST.

13

I'm sitting on the stile, Mary.

OLD SONG.

" Friends, Romans, Countrymen, lend me your ears."

ANTONY'S ADDRESS OVER THE DEAD BODY OF CÆSAR.

Her shape in dreams I oft behold,
And oft she whispers in my ear.

MOORE.

16

The Smith, a mighty man is he,
With large and sinewy hands,
And the muscles of his brawny arms,
Are strong as iron bands.

LONGFELLOW—
"THE VILLAGE BLACKSMITH."

17

" *The man that hath no music in himself,*
And is not moved with concord of sweet
sounds,
Is fit for treason, stratagems and spoils."

SHAKSPEARE

18

Beautiful i'le of the sea,
Sweet is thy mem'ry to me.

OLD SONG.

Lo, *how her dark arm holds me!—I am
     bound
By the soft touch of fingers light as leaves.*

ROBERT BUCHANAN.

PERSEUS ET CAPUT MEDUSÆ.

*The victor Perseus, with the Gorgon
        head,
O'er Lybyan sands his airy journey
        sped,
The gory drops distilled, as swift he
        flew,
And from each drop envenomed ser-
        pents grew.*

ANONYMOUS.

" *A woman moved is like a fountain
troubled,
Muddy, ill-seeming, thick, bereft of
beauty.*"

SHAKSPEARE.

BIRD SEED,

In process of germination.

It is an ancient Mariner,
  And he stoppeth one of three.
" By thy long grey beard and glittering eye,
  Now wherefore stopp'st thou me ?"

COLERIDGE.

THE TWINS.

She rose from her delicious sleep,
And put away her dark brown hair

WHITTIER—
"THE MAIDEN'S PRAYER."

26.

THE CARRIER DOVE.

Fly away to my native land, sweet dove,
Fly away to my native land,
And bear these lines to my lady love,
That I've traced with a feeble hand.

OLD SONG.

A hundred months have passed,
    Lorena,
Since last I held this hand in mine,
And felt thy pulse beat fast, Lorena,
    But mine beat faster far than
    thine.

            OLD SONG.

O have you seen fair Inez?
   She's gone into the West,
To dazzle when the sun goes down,
   And rob the world of rest.

HOOD

THE CHILD OF THE REGIMENT.

It is a wise father that knows his own son.

SHAKSPEARE.

'*How can I leave thee?*"

OLD SONG.

A gleaming shoulder cut the stream, and lo !
I saw the glistening Naiad rise :
She floated like a lily, white as snow,
With half-closed eyes.

ROBERT BUCHANAN.

I could a tale unfold   *   *   *   *

SHAKSPEARE.

"Yet in my dreams a form I view,
That thinks on me, and loves me
too;

I start, and when the vision's
flown,
I weep that I am all alone."

HENRY KIRK WHITE.

35

No: strike at once—my hour is come—
 in thee
I recognize the minister of Jove,
And, kneeling, thus submit me to his
 Power.

TALFOURD'S "ION."

Maud Muller, on a summer day,
Raked the meadow sweet with hay.
Beneath her torn hat glowed the wealth
Of simple beauty and rustic health.
Singing she wrought, and her merry glee
The mock-bird echoed from his tree.

WHITTIER.

But what is this?—it cometh—and it
   brings
A music with it—'tis the rush of wings.

EDGAR A. POE—
            "AL AARAAF."

Beneath the lamp the lady bowed,
And slowly rolled her eyes around.

COLERIDGE—

" CHRISTABEL."

" I'll chase the antelope over the plain,
    The tiger's cub I'll bind with a chain,
    And the wild gazelle, with its silvery
        feet,
    I'll give to thee for a playmate sweet."

                                OLD SONG.

"It is a beauteous lady, richly dressed,
  Around her neck are chains and
    jewels rare;
A velvet mantle shrouds her snowy
    breast,
  And a young child is sweetly
    slumbering there."

OLD SONG—

ALLAN PERCY.

41

"*What though the tempest madly raves?*
I dive into thy darksome caves,
And snatch the jewels hidden there,
To glisten in the upper air."

ANON—
"THE PEARL DIVER TO THE SEA."

"*Come one, come all; this rock shall fly*
From its firm base as soon as I!"

SCOTT.

'Twere vain to guess what shook the
    pious man,
Who looked not lovingly on that divan,
Nor show'd high relish for the banquet
    prest.

             Byron—
                  "The Corsair."

Oh, tell me some secluded place,
Where, weary with this fitful race,
These tired limbs awhile may rest.

AELLA GREENE.

The lone starry hour give me, love,
　　When still is the beautiful night,
When the round laughing moon I see, love,
　　Peep through the clouds, silver bright;
When the wind through the lone wood
　　　　sweeps, love,
　　And I gaze on some bright rising star,
When the world is asleep, wake thou, love,
　　And list while I touch my guitar.

OLD SERENADE

The " *poor but respectable parents.*"

OLD BIOGRAPHERS.

Oh, what a fall was there, my country-
men.

SHAKSPEARE.

List! 'tis a Grecian maid that sings,
While from Ilyssus' silvery springs,
    She draws the cool lymph in her
        graceful urn;
And by her side, in music's charm
        dissolving,
Some patriot youth, the glorious past
        revolving,
    Dreams of bright days that never
        can return.

                  MOORE.

Turn, Angelina, ever dear,
My charmer, turn to see
Thy own, thy long lost Edwin here,
Restor'd to love and thee!

GOLDSMITH—

"THE HERMIT."

"*My bark is on the Sea!*"

BYRON.

And there upon the moss she sits,
  The Dark Ladie in silent pain;
The heavy tear is in her eye,
  And drops and swells again.

COLERIDGE—
"BALLAD OF THE DARK LADIE."

"*The shades of night were falling fast,*
As through an Alpine village passed,
A youth, who bore, mid snow and ice,
A banner with the strange device,
    Excelsior !"

LONGFELLOW.

LAR

*Unbridled Spirit! throned upon the lap
Of ebon Midnight, whither dost thou
stray?*

ANON—
"HYMN TO THE NIGHT WIND."

The sullen bell is tolling,
That calls me to my doom.

FRANCES A. FULLER—
"QUEEN MARY'S LOVERS."

Thou art more wondrous fair than mortals
know.

*   *   *   *   *

Close up each eyelid with a warm, rich kiss,
    And let me listen while the sunlights go :
I cannot bear a time so still as this,
    Unbroken by thy voice's fall and flow.
Sing to me, Beautiful !—Sing low, sing
    low, sing low !

ROBERT BUCHANAN—
"THE SIREN."

O master! we are seven.

WORDSWORTH.

Hark! how the loud and ponderous mace
of time,
Knocks at the golden portals of the day.

LONGFELLOW—

"THE SPANISH STUDENT."

May is here, the delicate footed May,
  With her soft fingers full of leaves and flowers;
She brings a haunting wish to be away,
  Wasting in wood-paths the voluptuous hours.

N. P. WILLIS.

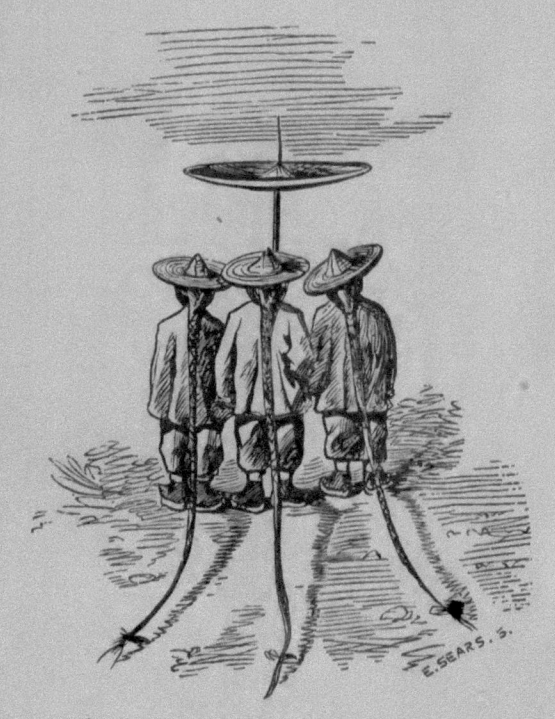